A Lamb for Lucy

Mary has been writing books for children and teenagers for fifteen years, and has now had more than 50 titles published. She writes funny stories, animal stories, spooky stories and romantic stories, and before she started *Lucy's Farm* she spent some time in Devon to be sure she got all the details right. Mary has two grown-up children and lives just outside London in a small Victorian cottage. She has a cat called Maisie and a collection of china rabbits. She says her favourite hobby is "pottering", as this is when she gets most of her ideas.

All of LUCY'S FARM books can be ordered at your local bookshop or are available by post from Book Service by Post (tel: 01624 675137).

LUCY'S FARM

A Lamb for Lucy

Mary Hooper

Illustrations by Anthony Lewis

MACMILLAN CHILDREN'S BOOKS

First published 2000 by Macmillan Children's Books
a division of Macmillan Publishers Limited
25 Eccleston Place, London SW1W 9NF
Basingstoke and Oxford
www.macmillan.co.uk

Associated companies throughout the world

ISBN 0 330 36794 3

Text copyright © Mary Hooper 2000
Illustrations copyright © Anthony Lewis 2000

1 3 5 7 9 8 6 4 2

A CIP catalogue record for this book is available from
the British Library

Phototypeset by Intype London Ltd
Printed and bound in Great Britain by Mackays of Chatham plc, Kent

Chapter One

"I'm worn out!" Lucy complained, flopping down at the long pine table in the kitchen.

"You'll feel better when you've eaten," her mum said. "Supper's all ready. Strap Kerry in her chair for me, will you?"

Lucy bent down to pick up her little sister from the floor. Kerry, who was almost a year old, biffed Lucy on the head and, as she was being put into her high chair, grabbed a handful of Lucy's long blonde hair.

"Ow!" Lucy said, laughing. "Monster!" She disentangled herself and sat down.

1

"I've helped Dad with the milking, fed the dogs, taken hay over to the calves *and* collected the eggs."

"What a treasure." Lucy's mum put a plateful of chicken casserole on the table. "And there's your reward. Tuck in. You don't have to wait for Dad."

Lucy started eating. She knew it was a supermarket-bought chicken and not one of their own, so at least she didn't have to worry that she was eating Amber or Chucky or another of her favourites.

Lucy Tremayne lived with her mum, dad and sister Kerry on Hollybrook Farm, just outside the village of Bransley in Devon. Bransley was near the coast and 6 miles from Honley, the nearest big town. Hollybrook was mostly a dairy farm, with about fifty Friesian cows. The family also had a flock of hens, several farm cats, two dogs and – new this year – half a dozen sheep with some lambs.

"And as well as doing all those jobs,"

Lucy went on between mouthfuls, "I've moved the last of my stuff from my bedroom to the hay barn. It looks fantastic up there now."

"I knew you'd love it once you'd moved in," her mum said, smiling.

When Lucy's mum and dad had broken the news to her that they were going to do Bed and Breakfast to earn extra money, Lucy had been appalled. Imagine having total strangers on the farm! They'd be wandering all over the place, touching the animals and probably feeding them all sorts of unsuitable stuff. And then when Lucy's dad had gone on to say that her nice, airy bedroom was needed for these strangers to sleep in, she'd been *horrified*.

Once it had been explained, though, that the top floor of the little hay barn next to the house would be cleared out and scrubbed and painted so that she could sleep there, Lucy had started to feel better. And now – well, she'd only moved into her new room a few days ago, but she loved it already. It was like being in a tree house, she thought, or having a flat of her own.

"When's the first one coming?" Lucy asked. "The first B and B person, I mean."

"The first *guest*," Julie Tremayne corrected her, mashing up a potato for Kerry, "will be here in ten days. He's a Mr Glen, and he's on some sort of business course in Honley."

There was a noise from the lobby – a couple of barks and a scuffle as two dogs landed on someone and were pushed away. "Get down!" Lucy heard her dad saying to the dogs. "You know you can't come in here."

Tim Tremayne opened the door to the kitchen, pushing back Roger and Podger as he did so. The dogs were part Labrador and part Border collie and when they weren't racing about outside, they lived in the boot lobby. They weren't allowed indoors properly because they were working dogs and usually covered in mud. That didn't stop them from trying to get in, though.

"I'm starving!" Lucy's dad said, smiling at the three faces looking up from the table, and brushing dirt and dog hairs off his corduroy trousers. He was a tall, good-looking man, with gingery-fair hair and a face that was tanned whatever time of the year it was. He went to the sink and washed his hands, while Lucy's mum opened the Aga, took out the last remaining portion of casserole and put it on the table.

Kerry, who'd seen the dogs put their noses round the door, started calling, "Woof . . . woof . . . woof . . ."

"Never mind woof – what about saying *Dad*?" Tim Tremayne said, patting Kerry's head. He started tucking into his food, and then paused and nodded at Lucy. "The sheep are doing well."

Lucy nodded eagerly, because she was the one who'd managed to persuade her dad to have sheep. "They're great, aren't they? Mind you, I took Kerry out to show her the lambs today but she wasn't a bit interested. She just turned away, plonked herself down on the grass and found a beetle to eat."

Her mum laughed. "I don't think she's going to be quite as animal mad as you."

"I was dying to get hold of a lamb and

cuddle it," Lucy went on longingly, "but Mr Mack said I shouldn't. He said if I put my scent on a lamb, its mother might reject it."

"Well, he should know," Lucy's dad said.

Mr Mackintyre owned Thorny Acres, the big farm just down the lane from Hollybrook. He was an expert on sheep and had a large flock of mixed breeds.

"The lambs are really fighting fit, though," Lucy added.

Her dad nodded. "It's just a pity they're all singles. I would have liked twins – two for the price of one, twins are."

"Well, maybe Shirley will have twins," Lucy said. Shirley was, so far, the only one of the six sheep they'd bought at market who hadn't had a lamb.

Her dad shrugged. "It doesn't look like it."

"Why not? What's your Shirley up to, then?" Lucy's mum asked, tucking a wisp of hair behind her ear. Her hair was the same colour as Lucy's but curly, and she had it on top of her head in an elastic band.

"Not much," Tim Tremayne sighed. "I don't reckon she's pregnant at all. We'll probably have to wait until next year to get her in lamb."

"They lamb so neatly," Lucy's mum mused. "I like the way they can eat grass at one end and drop a lamb at the other."

"That's the way to do it!" said Tim Tremayne. "No fuss and bother at all."

Lucy's mum raised her eyebrows and gave him a look.

"Do you think," Lucy said, "that Shirley looks at all the others with their lambs and thinks . . . hmm . . . isn't there something I'm supposed to be doing?"

Her mum and dad laughed. "I don't think sheep have got that much sense," said her dad.

"By the way, there's big news in the

village," Lucy's mum said suddenly, spooning food into Kerry's mouth.

"Oh yes," said Lucy's dad. "What's that, then? Someone trip over a kerb? Mrs Tregarth-Barton blow her nose?"

"No!" Lucy's mum laughed. "Apparently there's a gang of burglars doing the rounds of the big houses. A woman out at Widecombe Bay had her house broken into and all her jewellery taken."

"Well, that's all right, then," Tim Tremayne said. "They won't come here – you haven't *got* any jewellery that's worth anything."

"Now you're being silly," his wife scolded him. "We just ought to be aware." She turned to Lucy. "Keep your eyes open when you're going to and from school, love."

Lucy nodded. "And I'll tell Beth as well. We'll keep a look out."

Bethany Brown was Lucy's best friend.

They'd been friends for years and years – since they'd started at Bransley Mother and Toddler group together – and now they were both in the same class at the village school.

Lucy pushed away her empty plate and puffed out her cheeks. "That was lovely," she said. "And now I'm as full as a house."

She took her plate to the sink and looked out of the window. In the yard, one of the farm cats lay enjoying the last of the sun and ignoring Bertram, the perky little cockerel, who strutted past with his beak in the air. Faintly, from the nearby paddock, came a variety of baas and bleats. Mr Mack had told Lucy that each lamb had a distinctive call that the mother sheep could tell from scores of others, but Lucy wasn't sure she believed him.

"I think I'll go and check on the sheep before it gets dark," Lucy said suddenly.

"I know!" her mum said, grinning. "Anything to get out of the washing up!"

Lucy went to the door and pushed back Roger and Podger's noses, which had immediately appeared around it. "I'll be back to help you later."

"You'll be helping your dad," her mum said. "I'm going upstairs to finish the curtains in your old room ready for Mr Glen."

Lucy closed the kitchen door, pulled on her wellingtons and, with Roger and Podger bounding along beside her, went down the lane to the small paddock to look at the sheep.

They were over by the stream, and had five lambs playing beside them, jumping on and off a little hillock and seeing who was king of the castle. The sheep they'd named Shirley stood slightly apart from the others, seemingly very contented, nibbling at the grass.

"Come on, Shirley!" Lucy said under

her breath. "Where's your lamb? Aren't you going to have one?"

But Shirley said nothing. She just carried on chewing.

Chapter Two

"We've got to look out for a gang of burglars," Lucy said to Beth and Courtney as they left school together the following day.

"A gang of burglars!" Beth giggled. "What – will they be hanging about waiting to be spotted?"

"Will they have masks over their faces and a huge bag with 'SWAG' written on it?" Courtney put in.

Lucy felt herself going red. "Oh well, you know what I mean." She shot a glance at Courtney, who always seemed to be hanging about with them lately. Courtney hadn't been living in Bransley long and kept on all the time about how boring she found it, and how fantastic living in London had been. Sometimes Lucy wished she'd go back there.

It was Friday, and the following week was half-term. Lucy was looking forward to a whole week helping out at Hollybrook, sorting out her new room and getting to know the lambs a bit better.

"Are you going to walk home with me?" she asked Beth. "You know we've got the twin calves – you can help feed them if you like." Beth didn't live on a farm, but she loved animals nearly as much as Lucy did, and Lucy always let her share the baby animals.

But Beth shook her head and looked a bit embarrassed. "I said I'd go with Courtney to the library to choose a video."

"And then she's coming to my house to watch it," Courtney added, "and we're making our own pizza."

"Oh, right," Lucy said, going red again. What was going on? Beth nearly always came home from school with her on a Friday!

Lucy started chatting about the lambs and calves just to fill some awkward silences, and they soon reached the cross-roads by the war memorial, which was where she and Beth usually met and part-ed before and after school. Hollybrook Farm was to the right, down Embrook Lane, and Beth – and Courtney – lived further on, on the new estate.

"I'll see you in the week, then, Lucy," Beth said.

Lucy nodded. "Come round whenever you like." She shot a glance at Courtney and crossed her fingers. "You can come too, if you want. You can see the twin calves before they go to market."

Courtney shook her head. "I don't like things like cows." She shuddered. "Horrible, they are. And they smell."

15

"They don't!" Lucy protested.

"How would you know?" Courtney said. "You're too close to tell."

Lucy opened her mouth and shut it again. She didn't want to have a row with Courtney – mostly because she wasn't quite sure whose side Beth would be on – so she just shrugged, waved goodbye and went down Embrook Lane towards home. When she got to a puddle she stamped in it, pretending it was Courtney who was getting splashed.

By the time Lucy had reached Hollybrook, she felt better. She passed her dad, who was sluicing down the milking parlour ready for that afternoon's milking session, and went through the gate into the farm-yard. She looked up at the house and thought for the hundredth time how love-ly it was.

Hollybrook Farm was a big old house built of soft golden stone, with diamond-paned windows and a heavy pine door over which ivy and roses tangled. In honour of the B and B guests who were due to arrive shortly, Lucy's mum had placed pots of tulips and daffodils around the stone-flagged yard. This effect was rather spoilt, however, because the rest of the yard was taken up with pieces of rusty farm machinery, bales of hay, some old-fashioned milk churns, rubber tyres, a pile of wooden

chests and several old brooms and rakes –
not to mention a couple of dozen chickens
pecking around the place. Lucy's mum had
tried to tidy things up, but Lucy's dad
had objected.

"This is a working farm and this is how
it's *supposed* to look! Anyway, we need all
this stuff. And these things are in my
way," he'd added, moving the pots of
flowers into a corner. Later, Lucy's mum
had moved them back again.

Lucy went into the house for a glass of
orange and, with this in her hand and a
biscuit between her teeth, managed to
climb up the ladder to her room in the
hayloft.

She had homework to do. She'd much
rather have busied herself around the farm
with the animals, of course, but her mum
and dad insisted that homework came
first. Lucy didn't mind homework, but
liked it best when it was connected with
animals in some way, like when the class

had to find out about farming in Victorian times, or how a sheep's digestive system worked.

Her dad had brought a table over to the new loft room, and her old bed, but there wasn't much space for anything else, so all Lucy's books and papers were ranged along the low beams that ran the length of the room. It had been grotty in the little barn to start with: the floor had been littered with old grain sacks, the windows had been grimy, and a thick layer of dust and grass seed had lain over everything. Now, though, it was all scrubbed and bright, and Lucy's mum had made blue-checked curtains for the windows and bought a bright red rug for the floor.

Lucy did a page of history homework, then, bored, looked out of the window. From here she could see the big barn where the cows were, and the milking parlour, and, if she squashed herself right against the window, the edge of the sheep paddock down the lane. Mr Mack's farm with its surrounding fields was to the right, and further up the hill was the village – Lucy could just see the spire of the church and roofs of some of the village houses. Further down the road, she thought, Beth was at Courtney's house watching a video and eating pizza . . .

Low, steady moos from the milking parlour told Lucy that her dad had started on the milking. Lucy longed to be in there. Were there any new calves? Had her dad got the twins to drink from a bucket yet? Which cows and which calves were going to be sold at market next week?

Lucy sighed and reluctantly tore herself away from the window, trying to concentrate on kings and queens in Tudor times . . .

In the early hours of the morning, Lucy woke up to hear a noise from underneath her. Her first thought was that it was the burglars. Her heart started beating very fast and she was just about to dive under the duvet in fright when she heard her dad's voice.

"Lucy!" he was calling hoarsely. "Are you awake?"

Lucy crawled to the edge of the bed and pulled up the wooden trapdoor.

"What's the matter?" she called down. "What's going on?"

"I'm not sure," he said, "but there's been some strange noises over in the paddock. Want to come out with me?"

"You bet!" Lucy pulled on her jeans and boots, then put her woolly dressing gown on top and tied it tightly.

"I wouldn't get you up if it was a school day," her dad said, "but I know you're keen on anything to do with these sheep of yours."

Lucy climbed down the ladder. Her dad stood at the foot of it, fully dressed, carrying the big lantern he used to check up on the animals at night. "What time is it?" Lucy asked, excitedly, completely awake now.

"Just gone five," her dad said. "I was about to get up for milking when I heard a bit of a commotion coming from the paddock and wondered if it might be Shirley, lambing. I thought you could hold the light for me so we could see what's up. We might have to get the vet out."

Lucy, hurrying along beside her dad, looked up at him questioningly. "There's no noise now, though."

"It just stopped." He shrugged. "Maybe she won't need our help after all."

As they walked through the yard and came out onto the lane, the first pink streaks were beginning to show in the night sky. It was very cold and fresh, the grass and hedges wet with dew drops which glistened in the lamplight. In the stillness, one bird sang to announce the dawn.

Lucy sighed deeply. "It's all so . . . so beautiful and magical," she said.

"I always think this is the best time of the day," her dad agreed. "There's just me and the animals."

"And me as well, today!" Lucy said, straining to see ahead of them.

The sheep were in the paddock, inside the small pen they were put into last thing at night. They had some shelter from the weather here, and it stopped the new lambs wandering off and being found by foxes.

"I hope everything's all right," Lucy said anxiously.

"We'll soon find out," said her dad. And then he looked over into the pen and said, "*Oh, no!*"

Chapter Three

"What is it?" Lucy asked urgently, trying to see over the woven willow panels.

"It's poor old Shirley," said her dad. He opened the gate of the pen and they both went inside. "Move the other sheep and lambs out for me, will you, love?"

Lucy did so and, baaing and bleating, five sheep and their lambs fled to the other side of the paddock. Only Shirley remained – a motionless bundle of wool on the ground.

Tim Tremayne bent over her. "I'm afraid she's dead," he said after a moment.

"Oh, no, Dad!" Lucy gasped. One of

her lovely sheep . . . Suddenly feeling cold, she pulled her dressing gown more tightly around her. "What d'you think happened?"

"Difficult to say . . ." Lucy's dad handed her the lantern and gently rolled the dead sheep over so he could look at it more closely. "Well, what d'you know!" he exclaimed suddenly. "There's a lamb here! I nearly missed it."

"Really? Let me see!" Lucy forgot about Shirley for a moment and knelt down on the grass next to her father. She stared down at the tiny creature, which was still partly covered by the transparent bag it had been born in. "Oh! Can we . . . ?" Lucy began excitedly, but her dad interrupted her.

"It's no good, love. I'm afraid it's dead as well."

Lucy's eyes filled with tears. "Oh no! Do you think if we'd have got here earlier we might . . ."

"You can't tell," her dad said. He patted her shoulder. "These things happen on a farm, don't they? You know that by now."

Lucy bit her lip, trying not to cry.

"I thought there was something funny about Shirley," her dad said, straightening up. "I'm no expert, but maybe the lamb was lying wrongly inside her. Maybe it—"

Lucy suddenly gave a little cry. "I just saw the lamb move!"

Her dad took the lantern from her and held it high. "I'm afraid that's just wishful thinking, Lucy."

Lucy stared hard at the tiny, frail body of the lamb. Had she really seen it move, or had she imagined it?

While they were both watching, the lamb suddenly jerked its two back legs so that it broke free of the bag.

"Hey!" Tim Tremayne said. "You're right!"

There was an old towel hanging on the pen and Lucy quickly reached for it and wiped the lamb down. It was thin, damp and as small as a puppy – and very limp. It flinched and shivered under her hands, its eyes still closed.

Gently, Lucy picked up the lamb, rolled it in the towel and hugged it close to try and warm it. "Can I take it indoors?" she asked her dad breathlessly.

"Of course you can, love," he said. "But – well, it doesn't look too good."

"I've got to try, though!"

"Of course you've got to try. I just don't want you to get upset." Her father looked down at the small creature. "I'll be honest with you, love. It doesn't look to me as if that lamb is going to pull through."

"But I've *got* to try!" Lucy said again, as they hurried home.

Back at the house, all was quiet. Lucy's mum and Kerry were still asleep and even Podger and Roger seemed to know that it was too early to be leaping around making a noise.

"I don't know much about lambs," her dad said as they went into the kitchen, "but I guess you treat them the same as orphan calves – they need warmth and food more than anything. I don't know if that lamb is even strong enough to feed, though."

"I'm going to have to bottle-feed her, aren't I?" Lucy said. Holding the lamb gently in her arms, she moved a chair and sat down as close to the Aga as she could get.

Her dad shook his head doubtfully. "You've got a long job ahead of you, Lucy – and I'm not sure it'll work." He opened the oven door so that more warmth flooded out. "I'm going to have to leave you to it. If I hang about here much longer I'm going to get behind with the milking. Good luck, love."

He went out and Lucy, feeling shaky, loosened the towel that was round the lamb. She was almost too scared to look at it in case it had stopped breathing.

The lamb lay still and floppy on the towel, its breath coming in tiny gasps as if each one was an effort. Lucy patted and stroked it gently, trying to bring life back to its thin little legs, stimulate its circulation and warm its tiny body. She'd seen the sheep in the paddock licking their newborn lambs to do the same thing.

"Come on, you dear little thing," she said softly. "Get yourself going. You've got to try."

The lamb didn't move but Lucy persisted, massaging the little limbs and talking softly to it, urging it on. After some moments the lamb moved its head and made a slight noise.

Lucy was thrilled. "Are you looking for food?" she asked. If the lamb was hungry, Lucy knew that was a good sign. It meant it wasn't giving up – that it was trying to live. But how was she going to feed it? She knew there weren't any bottles from when Kerry had been a tiny baby, because her mum had fed Kerry herself. No, she'd have to go over and see Mr Mack. He would have had orphan lambs, so must have a feeding bottle.

Lucy took off her dressing gown and used it to make a bed for the lamb on the chair. "I'll be as quick as I can," she said, tucking it up into a cosy nest. "I'm going to try and get you some breakfast."

"You've got a *what*?" Mr Mack said.

"A lamb!" Lucy said breathlessly. She'd pulled on a couple of jumpers and run all the way to Thorny Acres. Although it was still very early, Mr Mack and his herds-man were just loading sheep into a lorry to go to market. "It's an orphan lamb and I've called her Rosie."

Mr Mack chuckled. He was a large

man – an old-style farmer with tweedy clothes and whiskery sideburns. "Why Rosie?"

"Just because she looks like a Rosie," said Lucy, who'd decided on the name while she was running down the lane. She hopped from foot to foot impatiently. "But I can't be long. I just wondered if you could lend me a bottle so I can feed her."

"Of course I can," Mr Mack said. He looked at Lucy consideringly. "But it might be easier if you let me have her. I've several orphans here. I can put her to one of my sheep who's lost a lamb."

"But it wouldn't take to her, would it?" Lucy said, puzzled. "I've seen them with strange lambs – they just push them away."

"Well, I could put the skin of a dead lamb on your Rosie," Mr Mack said. "The mother would take it all right, then."

Lucy wrinkled her nose. "She'll be all

right with me, thanks," she said. "I'm going to bottle-feed her and keep her warm and everything." She thought of the lamb snuggled under her dressing gown at home. "Oh, I hope she'll be all right!"

"I'd better get you that bottle then," Mr Mack said. He went into a barn and found a long glass bottle with a rubber teat on the top.

"Thanks, Mr Mack," Lucy said. Impatient to get back to Rosie, it was all she could do not to snatch the bottle and dash off. "I'll bring her over to meet you soon."

Mr Mack laughed. "That'll be a novelty. As if I haven't got two hundred lambs of my own!"

Lucy ran back to Hollybrook as fast as she could, clutching the bottle. "Run for Rosie . . . run for Rosie . . ." she puffed under her breath as she ran. Run to save Rosie's life!

*

"OK, then, Rosie," Lucy said, holding the lamb in her arms and offering the bottle of warm milk. "Here it is."

Rosie made a noise, too tiny for a bleat. She opened her mouth feebly, but didn't seem to understand about sucking. Lucy looked at her carefully, thinking that already she seemed a little better than when they'd found her. Her eyes were open now, and her body was warm. The curly wool of her coat was fluffy instead of being stuck to her damply.

Lucy tried with the bottle a few more times, and then she shook it gently into Rosie's open mouth so that milk dripped onto the lamb's tongue. Rosie seemed to get the message because she gulped at the drops, her eyelids fluttering.

"Come on, Rosie!" Lucy said. "You've got a whole bottle to get through here."

She shook some more milk into the lamb's mouth, and Rosie swallowed again.

"You're not getting it quickly enough,"

Lucy said, frowning. "You'll never build your strength up unless you eat properly." She smiled as she remembered her mum saying exactly the same thing to her. "Try a bit harder."

She pressed the teat onto Rosie's tongue so that a little milk escaped. Weakly, the lamb gulped and swallowed. Lucy persisted, trying again and again, and suddenly Rosie seemed to catch on, grasping the teat in her mouth, pulling her head back and swallowing the milk down.

Lucy heaved a sigh of relief. "Brilliant!" she cried. "Come on. Lovely milk. Have more!"

Rosie drank more of the milk, gulping and swallowing, and then fell asleep.

Lucy held up the bottle and looked at it. "Good girl!" she said. "You've taken nearly the whole lot." She couldn't wait to tell her dad. As for her mum – well, she didn't even know they had a lamb yet.

Lucy looked at the big old wooden clock on the wall. It was only seven-thirty. She'd saved a lamb's life and she hadn't even had breakfast!

Chapter Four

"Do you think she'll be all right now?" Lucy asked her dad on the afternoon of the following day. She yawned loudly, tired because she'd been up most of the night feeding Rosie.

Her dad nodded. "Thanks to you, I think she will be. She's looking pretty good to me."

"She is, isn't she?" Lucy said, and sighed with relief.

Lucy's dad had come back from the fields for a cup of tea, and the family were outside in the yard watching Rosie run about. Lucy had spent most of the past two days looking after the lamb, who'd needed feeding every couple of hours all the first day, and every three or so hours through the night. Lucy was just pleased it was half-term so the rules about bedtime could be relaxed a bit!

Rosie looked a hundred times better now. Her curly coat was a rich clotted-cream colour and soft as duck down, her eyes were bright and alert and her ears glowed peachy-pink inside.

"Oh, look at her now!" Lucy said, pointing and laughing. Rosie was looking up at them with her head to one side and a quizzical expression on her face, as if she knew she was being talked about.

"She's like a little puppy!" said Lucy's mum.

"Woof!" Kerry said, right on cue.

There was an answering bark from Podger. The two dogs were lying in the shadow of the old tractor, eyeing Rosie and just waiting for the command to "fetch".

"You two stay," Tim Tremayne called, glancing over to them. "We don't want this little one herded up just yet."

"Run across the yard so she can follow you," Julie Tremayne said to Lucy. "I like seeing the way her legs kick out at the back."

Lucy ran across the yard and Rosie followed her, with a hop, skip and a jump, bleating all the way and making three chickens scuttle for the safety of the hen coop.

"She's frolicking!" Lucy's mum said. "That's just what lambs are supposed to do."

"She didn't look much of a frolicker a couple of days ago," Tim Tremayne put in. "She looked dead."

"Oh don't, Dad!" Lucy groaned.

"It's true, love. And it just goes to show what a good job you've done with her. Look at her following you about! She thinks you're the mother sheep."

"But what's she going to do when you're back at school next week?" Lucy's mum asked. "That's what I want to know."

Lucy shrugged. "I suppose I could put her in with the other lambs. As long as you don't mind giving her a couple of bottles during the day, Mum."

"Ha!" her mum said. "Not only have I got a farm and a family to look after, now

I've got guests for Bed and Breakfast and a lamb to be fed on demand!"

"Either that or we make her into a nice sheepskin rug," Tim Tremayne suggested, grinning.

"Dad!" Lucy said, horrified. "What a terrible thing to say."

"Just a joke!" And Tim Tremayne laughed.

"But what am I going to do with you?" Lucy mused a few days later, looking at Rosie. "Dad was right – you think I'm your mum, don't you? I've even had to let you sleep downstairs in the hayloft." She bent down to hug the little lamb. "Beth will love you when she sees you!"

Lucy sighed. She'd been too busy with Rosie this week to go round to Beth's house, but she'd rung her once, wanting to tell her the news. Beth's mum had said she was at Courtney's, though. And she hadn't rung Lucy back.

"On Monday, I'll invite her home to meet you," Lucy said. And I won't invite Courtney, she thought to herself.

Rosie rolled over and over in the dusty yard, then spotted one of the cats and ran up to it. The cat disappeared into the shadows.

"You need someone to play with when I'm not here," Lucy said. She thought for a moment, and then, making up her mind all at once, she bent down to pick up Rosie. "So let's go and try you with the other lambs!"

Tucking Rosie securely under her arm, she went out of the yard and down the lane to the small paddock where the other Tremayne sheep were kept.

A shout of, "Hello, there!" came from across the fields and, shielding her eyes against the sun, Lucy saw Mr Mack coming towards her.

She waited by the hedge, Rosie squirming in her arms. It was the first time the lamb had been out of the farmyard, and Lucy was scared to put her down in the lane in case she ran off.

"That your orphan?" Mr Mack asked Lucy when he drew close.

Lucy nodded, proud as anything. "This is Rosie. Isn't she lovely?"

Mr Mack looked at her appraisingly. "She's a sturdy little thing. Should fetch a fair price at market."

"She's not going to market!" Lucy said, horrified. "You're as bad as Dad, you are – he wants to turn her into a sheepskin rug."

Mr Mack laughed. "That's farmers for you." He patted Rosie. "Looks like you've made a good job of her, though, lass."

Lucy beamed. "She's fine, now," she said. "I've got to go back to school on Monday, though, so I'm taking her into the paddock so she can make friends with some of the other lambs."

"That shouldn't be a problem," Mr

Mack said, and it seemed to Lucy that he was trying to hide a smile. "That is, unless your Rosie tries to get a milk supper from one of their mums." He twirled the knotted stick he carried. "I'm just off on my evening walk. You haven't seen a big white van hereabouts, have you?" Lucy shook her head and Mr Mack went on, "One of my shepherds said there was a white van parked over by the crossroads earlier. You can't be too careful these days."

"D'you mean because of the burglars? Are they still around, then?" Lucy asked.

"Could be . . . could be . . ." Mr Mack waved his stick in the air. "Just let them come near me, that's all."

Lucy grinned. Mr Mack was a very big man. If she was a burglar, she thought, she'd steer well clear of him.

Mr Mack went off down the lane. Lucy opened the gate to the paddock, stepped inside and put Rosie down on the grass.

The lamb stood there, legs splayed out, looking around her. Everything was fresh and new. Daffodils and purple crocuses mixed with pink clover and white daisies; lush green grass led towards hawthorn bushes thick with blossom.

The sheep and lambs already in the field eyed Lucy and Rosie and began to edge away from them.

"It's all right," Lucy said. "I'm not stopping. I just want you to be nice to Rosie."

Rosie put her head down on the grass, gave a short *baaaa!* then rubbed her face in the juicy green clover. "That's lovely stuff!" Lucy said to her. "You'll be eating lots and lots of it soon. But look over here . . ." She picked up Rosie and turned her round so that she could see the others. "Those are lambs, like you!"

Rosie stood very still, staring across the field.

"You're a lamb and they're lambs," Lucy said, hoping that Mr Mack wasn't around anywhere listening and laughing. "And these lambs are going to be your friends!"

Rosie gave a little bleat.

"At least, I hope they will," Lucy murmured. "But they won't come and talk to you while I'm here, so I'm going to leave you on your own for a little while."

Lucy gave Rosie one last pat and crept out of the field, then, heart in her mouth, waited on the other side of the hedge.

Rosie stood looking bewildered for a while, then ran backwards and forwards, searching for Lucy and baaing. It was all Lucy could do not to run in and snatch her up.

After a few moments, though, two of the lambs from the other side of the field ran towards Rosie. She hesitated for a moment, bleated a little and then took a few skipping steps towards them. The three lambs met in the middle of the field, sniffed each other and then ran, leaping and bounding, towards the stream.

Lucy breathed a sigh of relief. It looked as if Rosie had found some friends.

Chapter Five

"Are you coming straight home from school today?" Lucy's mum asked her the following Monday. Lucy, Kerry and their mother were in the kitchen, having breakfast, while Lucy's dad finished off that morning's milking.

Lucy nodded. "Of course – I've got to get back to Rosie as soon as I can. I'll be wondering how she is. This is the first full day I've had away from her."

Her mum smiled. "Now you know what we mums go through when we have to leave our babies!"

Lucy grinned, finished her cereal and

gave Kerry a finger of toast. "What time's the B and B man arriving?" she asked.

"Mr Glen's coming this evening," her mum said. "But I've got a hundred things to do before then – including going to market with your dad to have a look at some heifers."

Lucy nodded. She knew that when cows got too old to calve, they were sold at market and replaced by heifers – young cows who had yet to have their first calf and who could later be expected to give plenty of milk.

"Now, when you get in," her mum went on, "I want you to go and pick a couple of bunches of wild flowers from the hedges for Mr Glen's room."

Lucy raised her eyebrows. "He's having a bit of a fuss made of him, isn't he? New bed, new curtains, new carpet – and even flowers in his room!"

"It might sound silly to you," Julie Tremayne said, "but we need to make a go

50

of this Bed and Breakfast business, Lucy. The herd doesn't make what it used to and we've got to make the money up somewhere." She wiped Kerry's face, and Kerry spluttered and let out a wail. "I know you can be relied on to be polite to him at all times, Lucy – and to anyone else we've got staying here."

Lucy nodded. She got up and peered out of the window. Rosie was in the yard, edging close to one of the cats. Every time she got too near, though, the cat moved off, not wanting to play. Rosie had been put in the paddock with the other lambs for a few hours every day, but from now on, while Lucy was at school, she'd have to spend all day with them. In a moment Lucy was going to take her over there . . .

"See you soon," Lucy said to Rosie. She ruffled the little lamb's soft wool and then put her down on the grass. "I'll be back just after three o'clock. And

Mum will be over to give you a bottle later on."

As Rosie ran off to join the other lambs without a backward glance, Lucy slung her sports bag over her shoulder and picked up her rucksack. Back to school! Yuk! She'd much rather have stayed at home with Rosie – although she was looking forward to seeing Beth and to telling her and everyone else about the new lamb.

As Lucy walked up the lane towards the war memorial she wondered if Beth would be waiting there for her. She strained to see over the hedges . . . was that her in the distance? Was that two people waiting? Was Courtney there, too? She hoped not.

Lucy walked on quickly, later than usual because she'd had to give Rosie one last bottle before she'd taken her over to the paddock. Ahead of her, swallows wheeled and swung through the sky, twittering and calling to each other. It really was spring, Lucy thought happily. Time, soon, for the cows to be turned out of their winter quarters and let loose to enjoy the freedom of the fields.

"Baaaa!" There was a faint bleat from somewhere behind her, and Lucy frowned. As far as she knew, there were no sheep in the nearby fields.

"Baaaa!" It was closer this time, and although Lucy had thought that she wouldn't be able to tell one bleat from another, to her that sounded very much like . . .

She stopped, put down her bags and climbed onto a gate to see better.

"Oh, no!" she gasped. It was Rosie, charging along the lane as fast as her furry little legs could carry her. "How did you get out of the paddock?"

Rosie ran up to Lucy, baaing all the way. Lucy didn't know whether to scold her or hug her.

"You naughty thing!" she said, scooping her up. "You've escaped and come after me!" She cuddled the little lamb. "I've got to go to school, though. I can't stay at home and play with you today!"

In the distance, Lucy heard the first bell ringing. This was the one which told everyone that school would be starting in five minutes.

"What am I going to do with you?" Lucy chewed her lip, worried. She couldn't just leave Rosie in the lane. And she wouldn't be safe just plonked over the hedge into the nearest field, either. Especially as she seemed so determined to follow Lucy.

"Baaaa!" Rosie put in.

"What am I going to do?" Lucy said again. "I haven't got time to take you back home now and Mrs Fern will be cross if I'm late!"

The second bell rang. Rosie pawed at Lucy's sports bag – and all at once Lucy had an idea. It was a bit mad, but she had to do something. She picked up Rosie, popped her inside the sports bag and half-zipped it up. Rosie, willing to play along, lay down flat on Lucy's sports kit, seeming to think it was some sort of game.

Lucy, holding the bag carefully, began to hurry along the lane, past the war memorial and towards school. There was no one around now, so Beth and Courtney had obviously gone without her.

"I don't know what I'm going to do with you, Rosie," she puffed, "but I'll think of something. Maybe I can hide you in one of the sheds. You've just got to go to sleep and keep quiet!"

She nibbled her lower lip as she ran. She'd done a daft thing, she knew that, but it was too late now. Lucy's lamb was going to school!

Chapter Six

In Class 5, everyone was talking at once. They'd had a message to say that Mrs Fern was busy in the staffroom and would be five minutes late to take Register, so they were supposed to be sitting quietly and putting the last-minute touches to their half-term homework.

They were doing nothing of the kind, of course. Five girls were singing, pretending they were in a band, three boys were playing football with an orange, and the rest of the class were telling each other what they'd been doing in their week off.

Lucy had stowed her sports bag

carefully under the desk she shared with Beth, and was waiting for the right time to tell her what was in it.

"I'm sorry I didn't come round to your house," Beth was saying. "My gran came, and then my mum took me into town shopping, and then—"

"And then one day you came round to see me, didn't you?" Courtney put in. She'd moved tables, Lucy noticed. Now she was sitting right behind them. "We used up all my mum's nail varnish on our toes!"

Beth nodded a bit uneasily. "What did you do all week, Lucy?" she asked. "How are the calves?"

Lucy shifted in her seat and glanced down to the sports bag. "The calves are fine. At least, I think they are," she said. "I've been a bit busy with something else."

Beth's eyebrows lifted. "What?"

"Don't tell us – more smelly animals!" Courtney sneered.

Lucy ignored her. "I don't know if you remember – we had one sheep that hadn't had a lamb," she said to Beth. "Well, just when we'd decided she couldn't have been pregnant, she had the lamb and then died."

Beth's eyes widened. "Oooh," she said sympathetically. "Is the lamb all right, though? Did you save it?"

Lucy nodded. "I had to bottle-feed her all through the first night, though. Every three hours! She's all right now – she's gorgeous! I've called her Rosie."

"Aaaahh!" Beth said. "Can I come and see her?"

"Course you can," Lucy said. "You can have a go at feeding her if you like."

Courtney was silent.

"As a matter of fact," Lucy added, lowering her voice, "you can see her now if you want to."

"What? What d'you mean?"

"I've got her here, under my desk!" Lucy whispered. "She followed me to school and I didn't have time to take her home again."

"No!" Beth gasped. "You haven't *really*?"

Lucy giggled. "I know it's mad but I couldn't think of what else to do. I thought that after Register I'd take her out to the sports shed while everyone's changing for gym and leave her in there until Break. And then . . . I don't know . . . I thought I'd make some excuse about having to pop home for something and take her back."

"Is she in there?" Beth was looking under the desk at the sports bag in amazement. "Is she all right?"

"I think she's asleep," Lucy said. "She sleeps quite a lot and . . ."

But Beth had dropped to her hands and knees under the desk and was already delving into the bag. "Ooohh! She's gorgeous!" she said. "Oh, can she come out so I can give her a cuddle!"

"I don't really want to get her out," Lucy said anxiously. "She might be frightened with everyone around. And I don't want Mrs Fern to find out she's here."

Rosie suddenly lifted her head and looked around her, quite happy to be in a sports bag surrounded by desk legs and children's ankles.

Beth shrieked with laughter. "Oh, look! She's so sweet!"

"What a dumb thing to do!" Courtney said suddenly. "Fancy bringing a lamb to school. The things some people do to get noticed."

"She followed me!" Lucy said crossly. "I didn't have any choice."

The classroom door opened and Lucy quickly shook Beth's shoulder for her to get up. "It's Mrs Fern!" she hissed.

Beth got to her feet, her face wreathed in smiles. "She's so lovely! She's all warm and fluffy!"

"Ssshhh!" Lucy said.

As Mrs Fern closed the door and sat down at her desk, everyone fell silent. More or less.

"Sorry I was late," Mrs Fern said. "But let's quickly get through the Register and then you can all go along to the Hall for gym." She looked round. "And I'd like complete quiet before I start, please."

There was silence from every child. From underneath Lucy's desk, though, there came a loud bleat. As everyone looked round, startled, Lucy put her hand over her mouth.

Mrs Fern looked up, frowning. "And whoever is playing the fool can stop it straight away."

She read out ten names.

"Baaa!" came again.

"I don't think this is funny," Mrs Fern said, looking up. "Is that you, Lucy?"

"No," Lucy said. "It's not me. That is, not exactly."

"What do you mean?"

"Not me, but . . ." As Lucy floundered, wondering what to say, Courtney suddenly burst out. "She's got a lamb under her desk, Miss!"

"Baaaa! Baaaa!"

Shouts, giggles and confusion broke out around the class. Those near to Lucy made a dive under her desk, and those on the other side of the classroom jumped up in order to see better. Everyone started talking at once.

Looking cross, Mrs Fern clapped her hands several times. "Sit down!" she shouted. "Everyone sit down!" After some minutes, when everyone was back in their places, she looked at Lucy and said quite sternly, "And now, Lucy, I suggest you tell me exactly what is going on."

Chapter Seven

Ten minutes later, Lucy was hurrying back down the lane to Hollybrook Farm, holding Rosie securely under her arm.

"Mrs Fern was all right, really," she said to Rosie. "I mean, she was a bit surprised. But when I explained . . ."

She hugged the lamb. "But didn't everyone make a fuss of you! And I had to tell them all about when you were born, and how you had to be bottle-fed, and then everyone wanted to hold you . . ."

She stopped by a gate and held the lamb up in front of her, its legs dangling. "But you mustn't do it again!" she said, trying to sound strict. "And I'm going to get Dad to look round the paddock fence tonight and discover how you got out."

Rosie opened her mouth wide so that Lucy could see two rows of white teeth and a pink tongue. "Baaa!"

Lucy giggled. Who could possibly be cross with a lamb? Especially one as lovely as Rosie.

A beaten-up Landrover came down the lane towards Lucy and stopped with a squeal of brakes. "What are you up to, lass?" Mr Mack asked, leaning out of the driver's seat. "I never see you without that lamb lately. And aren't you supposed to be at school?"

"She came to school with me," Lucy said, grinning. "She followed me. I'm just taking her home again."

Mr Mack roared with laughter. "Followed you to school?" he said. "There's a thing. What would happen if my lambs followed me about? Think of a couple of hundred coming down to the Dog and Duck on a Sunday lunchtime!"

Still laughing, he drove off. Lucy hoisted Rosie into a more comfortable position and carried on towards the farm. She knew her mum and dad would be out, so she was going to shut Rosie in the haybarn and leave a note.

When she got to the farm, Lucy was

surprised to find the five-bar gate open, but thought that maybe her parents had been in a rush to get to the market so as not to miss the first sales.

And then a man appeared from behind the chicken coop.

A man she'd never seen before.

Lucy gasped. "Who are . . ." she began, and then she realized who it must be. Of course! Mr Glen! Their very first Bed and Breakfast guest, who was arriving today.

"Oh, are you Mr Glen?" Lucy asked. Not waiting for a reply, she hurried on. "Mum and Dad are out – I'm very sorry. Mum wasn't expecting you until this evening – she'll be really cross she wasn't here to meet you."

The man opened his mouth and shut it again.

"Did you get an earlier train or something?" Lucy asked. "Would you like to be shown to your room? I'm sure it's all ready." Lucy's mind went into overdrive.

She knew her mum and dad wouldn't be home until midday, and that her mum had been really bothered about making Mr Glen feel welcome. "If you want to get your suitcase in, I'll make you a cup of tea," she offered.

"That would be nice. Just what the doctor ordered," the man said, smiling. "And I'd love to see my room."

Lucy got the spare key from under the big seashell where it was always kept. Still carrying Rosie, she led the way in through the boot lobby, which was empty because Roger and Podger had also gone to market. "This is my pet lamb, by the way," she said. "I mean, I don't usually walk around with a lamb, but she came to school with me and I had to bring her home." She glanced at the man, thinking that he didn't have much to say for himself. "Just as well, really, otherwise you would have been waiting around all morning."

"Nice room," the man said, looking

around the kitchen appraisingly. "Lovely old pine table."

Lucy nodded and put Rosie down on the floor, out of harm's way. She put the kettle on the top of the Aga and went into the pantry to get the tea tin. "Would you prefer coffee?" she called politely. There was no reply, and she turned to see what Mr Glen was doing.

But Mr Glen was nowhere to be seen. As Lucy took a step forward, the pantry door was suddenly slammed in her face. There was the sound of the key being turned in the lock.

"What's going on?" Lucy cried, startled. "What are you doing?"

There was no reply, just the sound of someone running upstairs to the bedrooms – and a *baaa* from Rosie, outside in the kitchen.

All at once Lucy realized the awful truth. It's not Mr Glen! she thought, shocked. And if it isn't him . . .

"Let me out!" she shouted. She began to bang on the pantry door. "Let me out at once! You're not Mr Glen at all! You're a burglar, aren't you?"

Not surprisingly, she didn't get a reply – except from Rosie.

"Baaa!" she heard. "Baaa-aaa!"

"Oh, are you all right, Rosie?" Lucy called desperately. Suppose Rosie hurt herself – jumped up on the stove or something? Suppose the man hurt her?

She heard him come back down the stairs, heavy boots clattering. Was he carrying something? Was he bringing things – things he'd stolen – downstairs?

"Let me out!" Lucy shouted, rather hopelessly. She heard the man go into the sitting room – no doubt to try and see what he could take from there. There was a fainter bleat from the direction of the hall.

"Rosie!" Lucy called urgently. She didn't want her to go near the man. Suppose he was dangerous?

Oh no! Lucy sank down to the floor. What an idiot she'd been. What were her mum and dad going to say when they found out that she'd actually let a burglar in and made him welcome? Oh, how could she have been so stupid as to just presume he was Mr Glen?

"Baaa!" came several times, and then there was a sharp, startled kind of bleat, as if Rosie had suddenly been stopped from making a sound.

"Rosie!" Lucy shouted, feeling frightened. "Are you all right?"

There was no reply, just the sound of the man moving around the house – stealing, Lucy thought, all their things. Maybe everything they had! And what had he done with Rosie?

Lucy jumped to her feet. "Let me out!" she shouted again, banging on the door for all she was worth. "Let me out at once!"

But no one came.

Chapter Eight

Lucy pressed her ear against the pantry door, listening intently. Was the man outside now or was he in the dining room, stealing their best silver knives and forks? More importantly, where was Rosie? What had the man done with her?

She looked round the pantry, which had rows of shelves containing jars, tins, packets and bowls. Food, food everywhere. However long she was shut in, at least she wouldn't starve. There was a window with a fixed wire-mesh covering, but it was much too tiny for her to climb through. If Rosie was in here with her, Lucy thought, she might have been able to do what peo-ple did in stories – prise off the wire and put Rosie out of the window with a note tied round her, asking for help. She didn't know where Rosie was, though. She nib-bled her lip anxiously. Oh, let her be all right!

Lucy glanced up at the window again. She moved some jars of jam and mar-malade out of the way and climbed up on a shelf to try and see what was going on. It was no good, though, the holes in the mesh were just too small to see through. Putting her mouth close to it she shouted, "Help!" and then, "Help, I'm locked in!" until she was hoarse.

What time was it? she wondered. Would her mum and dad come back from market straight away, or would they go shopping first? Back at school were they wondering what had happened to her? Would Mrs Fern be cross?

Lucy climbed off the shelf and rubbed

her knees. It was cold in the pantry. How long was she going to be in here? It already seemed like hours. What was that man doing now? Where was Rosie?

Suddenly she heard faint sounds. The man was talking to someone. Lucy hadn't heard anyone arrive, though, so perhaps he was speaking into a mobile phone.

"Ready, Stan," she heard the man say. "Drive up now. I've got all the stuff ready to move."

Of course! she thought. There were two of them. Someone had been sitting in a van hidden somewhere down the lane.

There was the noise of a big vehicle driving into the yard.

"Let me out!" Lucy screamed at the top of her voice. "Help! Thieves!"

Suddenly, just as she felt she was going to burst into tears of fury and frustration, she heard another vehicle race into the yard at top speed. And then another and another. There were sirens going and men's voices shouting.

Lucy stayed quiet for some moments, working out what was going on, and then she began calling again and thumping on the door. "I'm in the pantry – through the kitchen. Help! I'm locked in."

She heard someone come into the kitchen. "Over here!" she called, and was thrilled to hear an answering "Baaaa!"

"I'm locked in the pantry!"

The key was turned in the lock, the door was opened – and there stood Mr Mack, with Rosie under his arm.

Lucy hugged him – hugged the two of them. "Oh, Mr Mack, thank you!" she said, feeling weak with relief. "Where did you find Rosie? What's going on? Have the police caught that man? Oh, is Rosie all right?"

"Well, now," Mr Mack said, smiling. "One question at a time, lass, if you please."

*

The last police car had driven away, well pleased to capture red-handed the two burglars who had caused so much trouble in the area. At that moment Lucy's mum and dad had returned home. Kerry had been put down for a nap while Lucy explained her side of the story, and everyone was sitting at the kitchen table having a large pot of tea. Rosie had been given a bottle and was curled up like a cat under Lucy's chair.

"And then," Lucy finished telling the story and beamed at her hero, "Mr Mack came and rescued me!"

Lucy's mum put an arm around her daughter's shoulders and squeezed her tightly. "You did very well, love," she said. "I'm just so relieved that you're all right." She smiled at Mr Mack. "We've got to thank our lucky stars that you came along and realized what was going on."

"Well, I knew something must be up," Mr Mack said. "I'd seen Lucy with that pet lamb of hers a bit earlier, and then what should I see but it come galloping along the lane towards me on its own!"

"And what did you do then?" Lucy's dad asked.

"Well, I picked up the lamb to bring it back to Lucy, but when I got near the house I heard her inside, shouting for all she was worth about burglars and being locked in." Mr Mack chuckled. "It was a wonder they couldn't hear her in the village! I got a glimpse of one of the rogues at the window, cut back across the fields to phone the police, and – well, you know the rest."

Tim Tremayne clapped an arm around Mr Mack. "I do, and I'm very grateful to you."

"You should be grateful to that lamb of yours, really," Mr Mack said. He scratched his side-whiskers. "Blow me, it was almost as if the creature came haring down the lane to find me."

"I think that's just what she was doing!" Lucy said.

Her dad grinned at her. "So your rescue lamb rescued *you*."

Lucy picked up Rosie and hugged her. "I knew she was special."

"Guess we won't make her into a rug after all, then," her dad said.

"Just you try!" Lucy's mum cleared the cups away. "I hate to say this, Lucy," she went on, "but I really think you ought to be getting back to school. They'll be wondering what's happened to you."

"I suppose so," Lucy said reluctantly, thinking that school was going to seem terribly boring after this.

Just as she was about to give her mum instructions for keeping Rosie in until she'd gone out of sight, Roger and Podger began barking in the yard. A moment later, there was a tentative tap on the kitchen door. "Excuse me . . ." a voice said, and a man's face appeared round it. "I think I'm a bit early . . ."

Everyone looked in his direction.

"I'm Mr Glen," the man said – and wondered why everyone burst out laughing.

LUCY'S FARM 2
Lucy's Donkey Rescue

When Lucy meets a poor neglected donkey on the beach, she is desperate to help him. His horrible owner is so cruel.

Lucy knows that her parents will never agree to keeping another animal on the farm. Can Donald, a very clever donkey, prove that Hollybrook really does need him?

LUCY'S FARM 3
Frankie's Badger Cub

Lucy and her friend Beth enjoy watching the badgers in the woods. They are horrified to find one day that all the badgers have gone – except for one little cub.

But there are more mysteries down in the woods. Someone has been living in the old ruined cottage. Can Lucy discover what is going on – and save her little badger cub?

LUCY'S FARM 4
A Stormy Night for Lucy

Lucy is very fond of Buttercup, a cow which her father has just bought. Lucy can't wait for Buttercup's calf to be born!

But when the calf is due, a terrible storm traps Lucy's parents miles from home. And now Buttercup is in trouble. Scared and alone, Lucy knows that only she can bring the tiny calf safely into the world . . .

LUCY'S FARM 5
Lucy's Wild Pony

Lucy doesn't believe the spooky stories she hears about ghosts on the moors. Everyone knows that only wild ponies live up there!

Following a friend who has wandered too far on the moor, Lucy finds herself in great danger. But then a mysterious white pony appears . . .

Collect all the LUCY'S FARM books!

The prices shown below are correct at the time of going to press. However, Macmillan Publishers reserve the right to show new retail prices on covers which may differ from those previously advertised.

Mary Hooper

A Lamb for Lucy	0 330 36794 3	£2.99
Lucy's Donkey Rescue	0 330 36795 1	£2.99
Frankie's Badger Cub	0 330 36796 X	£2.99
A Stormy Night for Lucy	0 330 36797 8	£2.99
Lucy's Wild Pony	0 330 36798 6	£2.99
Lucy's Perfect Piglet	0 330 36799 4	£2.99

All Macmillan titles can be ordered at your local bookshop or are available by post from:

**Books Service by Post
PO Box 29, Douglas, Isle of Man IM99 1BQ**

Credit cards accepted. For details:
Telephone: 01624 675137
Fax: 01624 670923
E-mail: bookshop@enterprise.net

Free postage and packing in the UK.
Overseas customers: add £1 per book (paperback)
and £3 per book (hardback)